A Thousand Words

by Vidas Barzdukas
illustrated by Marilee Harrald-Pilz

HOUGHTON MIFFLIN HARCOURT
School Publishers

Copyright © by Houghton Mifflin Harcourt Publishing Company

Printed in China

ISBN-13: 978-0-547-01896-6
ISBN-10: 0-547-01896-7

2 3 4 5 6 7 8 0940 18 17 16 15 14 13 12 11 10

Matilda leaned against the oak tree, deep in thought. Across the field, one of her classmates huffed and puffed as he ran to second base during a game of kickball. Matilda barely noticed him. She was busy watching a bird up in the sky. Then she scribbled in her notebook:

Bluebird, bluebird
Up in the sky
Where are you going?
Where do you fly?

Matilda smiled to herself. She loved writing poetry. She loved the way the words flowed from her mind onto the page.

Matilda spent hours alone in her bedroom writing poems whenever she could. She wrote about whatever she was thinking. Once she wrote about her baby brother crying in his nursery. She even wrote a poem about the back door banging during a storm.

However, Matilda never shared her poems with anyone. It was her secret. She was afraid her friends and family would laugh at her or think her poems were silly. Her notebook was like her own private museum of poems that only she could visit.

One day, Matilda was walking to math class when she heard a voice behind her.

"Hey, Matty!" called out her friend Liz. "I think you dropped something!"

Matilda turned around. She started to shake. Liz stood holding one of Matilda's poems. It must have fallen out of her notebook! Not only that, but Liz was actually reading the poem!

"Give me that!" exclaimed Matilda, reaching out. She tore the page from Liz's hand. "That's mine! Stop reading it!"

"But I thought it was—" began Liz.

"I don't care!" said Matilda, stomping away.

The next day, Matilda sat alone in the cafeteria, eating her sandwich. Her green notebook was hidden deep inside her backpack. She had wrapped a rubber band around it to make sure nothing would fall out. She looked up and saw Liz approaching. Her friends Alice and Juan were with Liz, too. Matilda's heart sank.

"Hi, Matty," said Liz. "I told Alice and Juan about your poem."

"Oh, really?" said Matilda, trying to sound calm. "That's nice."

"I thought it was cool," said Liz. "You're a really good writer."

"Liz told me about your poem," said Alice. "It sounded neat."

Matilda was stunned. She stared at her three friends. They liked her poems?

"Why didn't you share your poems with us before?" asked Juan. "I like to draw. Maybe I could draw a picture for one of your poems."

Matilda didn't know what to say.

"That's a great idea!" said Alice. "I've written a couple of poems. Can you draw pictures for those, too?"

"Sure!" said Juan. "I can draw pictures for both of you."

Matilda put down her sandwich. "Wait a second," she said slowly. "You write poetry, too?" Alice and Liz nodded. "Can I read some of it?" asked Matilda.

"Sure," said Liz. "Alice and Juan are coming over after school tomorrow. You should come along, too."

The next day, the four friends met at Liz's house to read one another's poetry. While they read, Juan drew pictures. Matilda smiled as she read. Her friends shared her love of writing. And they wrote just as much as she did.

"I have an idea," said Matilda when they were finished. "Why don't we put together a poetry magazine?"

"That's a great idea!" said Liz.

"I can draw the cover!" added Juan.

The four friends began working on their poetry magazine. Each one had the same number of poems in the magazine. Juan's uncle worked at the copy store, so he helped them negotiate a price with the printer. However, the magazine still cost money to make. They decided the only solution was to charge one dollar per copy.

Two weeks later, several cardboard boxes arrived at school. Matilda and Liz ripped open the first box. Inside were copies of their magazine. It was called *A Thousand Words*.

Matilda picked up the magazine and studied it. The cover was smooth and glossy. It looked like a real magazine. Matilda smiled to herself. Writing poetry had always been her special secret. "Maybe some secrets should be shared with everyone," she thought.

Responding

Story Structure

What happens in the story? What is the
problem? How is the problem solved?
Copy the chart below. List the problem,
events, and solution in the boxes.

Problem: Matilda is afraid to share her poetry.	Solution: ?
Events: ?	

✏ Write About It

Text to Self Matilda loves poetry. What
do you like to read? Write a paragraph
about what you like or do not like to read.
Make sure to explain why you feel the
way you do.